Jelly Bean Dean
and the
Bubble Machine

Jo Zoë & Bridger

May all your days be filled
with lots & lots of Bubbles...

Tracy Stanaway

Fulton Books, Inc.
Meadville, PA

Published by Fulton Books 2021

ISBN 978-1-64654-828-6 (paperback)
ISBN 978-1-63860-050-3 (hardcover)
ISBN 978-1-64654-829-3 (digital)

Printed in the United States of America

Jelly Bean Dean

and the

Bubble Machine

TRACY STANAWAY

All summer long, Jelly Bean Dean had been walking along the beach, picking up special things—beautiful, unique shells, starfish, sand dollars, and more. Every day, she would come home and show her mommy her treasures!

"Wow, Jelly Bean," her mom said, "one never knows what they will find on the beach!"

On the very last day of her summer vacation, Jelly Bean couldn't stand it! She had to go out on one more treasure hunt. She was getting discouraged looking for her last treasure when she finally saw it. It practically tripped her—it was so close. It was the most unusual little machine that looked like it had little holes all around it. *Gosh*, thought Jelly Bean Dean, *this little machine is special. I better leave it here. Somebody must be missing it*. Giving it one last longing look, Jelly Bean started for home.

As she was walking, though, she had the funniest feeling that something was following her. Turning around quickly and a little frightened, she saw the funny little machine flying toward her in the wind. *Wait, though*, she thought, *the air is perfectly still. No wind today.*

Warily, she started walking faster. The machine started flying faster. She started running. The machine was flying even faster. Suddenly, Jelly Bean Dean was swirling around with the machine and couldn't stop! When she finally landed in a heap in the sand, the funny machine was right overhead with beautiful bubbles coming out of all the holes in it. Strangely enough, it continued to follow her all the way home.

With school starting the next day, Jelly Bean had a lot of things to put in her backpack. Tissues, markers, and notebooks went into her backpack. When she tried to put her lunchbox in it the next morning, it wouldn't fit! Peering inside her backpack, she noticed the funny little bubble machine was in there. *Hmmm*, thought Jelly Bean, *I'm pretty sure I didn't put it in there. Guess, it's coming to school with me!*

Jelly Bean put her things from her backpack in their place at school but left the machine in her new blue backpack. As Ms. P Bean was starting the first lesson of the morning, all of a sudden, everyone heard a terrible rattling and knocking noise coming from Jelly Bean Dean's backpack. Then it happened. Her backpack burst open, sending flying bubbles all over the room. In the middle of the ceiling was the beautiful bubble machine sending bubbles everywhere!

"Did you see that?" said a boy bean.

"What was that?" exclaimed another bean.

"Oh my, my, my!" said Ms. P Bean. "Where did all those flying bubbles go? I can't see any of them anymore."

"Um, Ms. P Bean," said Rose Bean, "there's a bubble with a spider in it on your shoe!"

"Eeeek!" Ms. P Bean started shrieking. "Get it off! Get it off!"

One very brave bean tried to be the hero and get it off, but the bubble popped, and the very big spider just jumped and landed right above the projector. Ms. P Bean was terrified of spiders that made it very hard to teach the rest of the morning with the spider watching her.

17

After lunch, strange things began happening in the classroom. The bubble machine started shaking again, sending bubbles, hovering above each of the student's heads. Then it happened. The bubbles all popped, and the items in them landed on all the beans. Chaos was everywhere. When the flourish of activity was over, each bean discovered that the thing they were the most afraid of was right in front of them.

The machine stopped right over Jelly Bean Dean but, this time, inside a giant huge bubble was a note. Jelly Bean Dean popped it and read it.

Ms. P Bean's class read the note that is passed.

Listen up, no wiggling, and be a good little class. No freaking out, and on your face not a pout. Once you've read me, you'll figure it out. No tears can be shed while this note is read, so put your listening caps very tight on your head.

Ms. P Bean, I better start with you, I heard you scream, and your face turned blue when I quite accidentally landed on your shoe. I'm just a wee bug. I can't hurt a flea. I'll protect you from harm, just wait and see.

Jelly Bean Dean, in front of you see is the word "perfect," which you don't have to be.

If you just do your best with a worker bean's heart, you'll know you're off to a very good start.

In front of you, Rose, is a weird-looking clown. Don't be afraid when you see one in town. Just look at him closely and imagine his face as a beautiful butterfly just flittering in space.

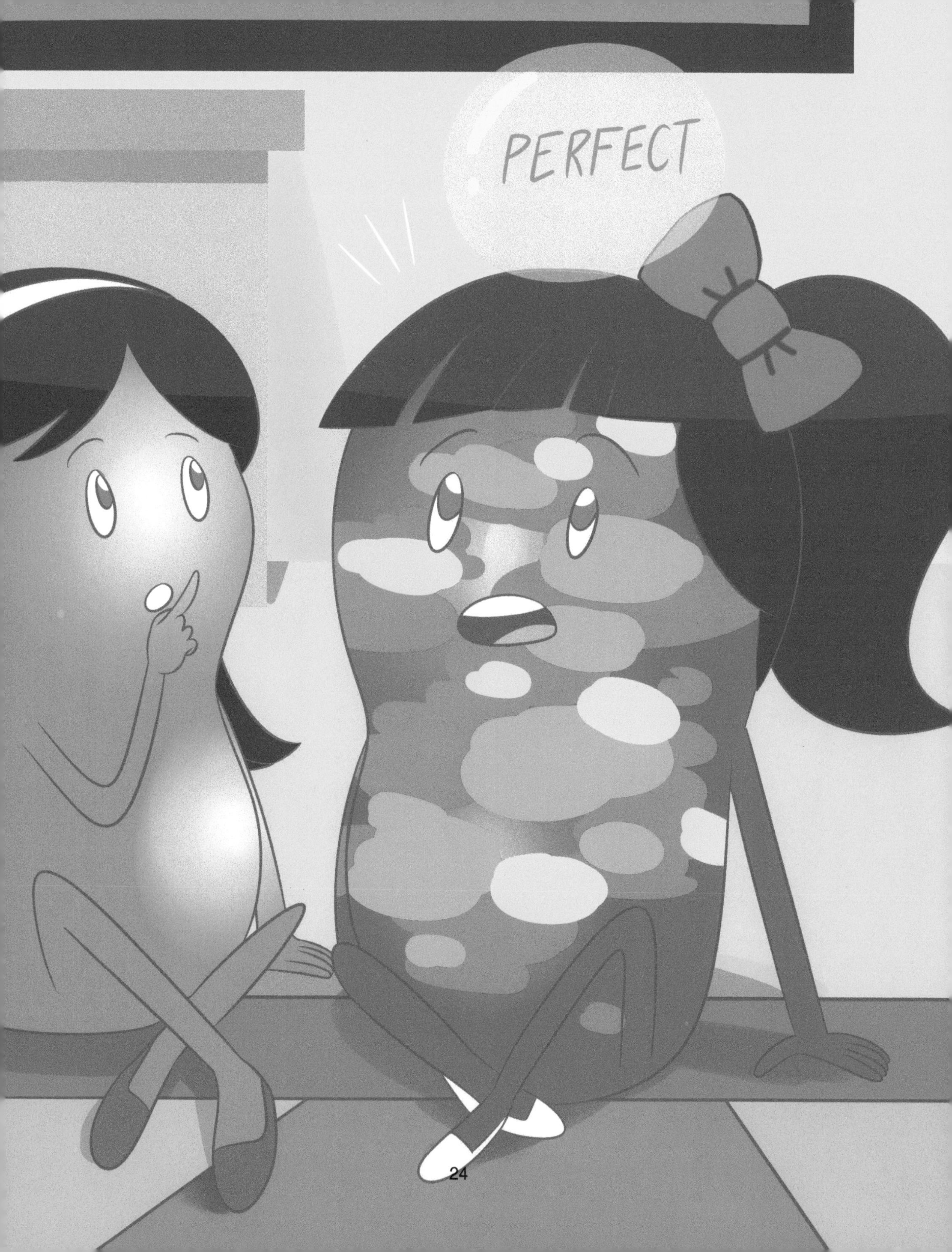
PERFECT

Oh, Ms. P's class, don't you see it can be, that whatever you're afraid of just set it free. A quick thought in your head, a short fleeting tick, don't hold it inside, get it out quick.

I'm packing up your fears back inside of this thing. I'll keep them safe inside this machine. They're comfy in here, and if they shout, I promise you, I'll never let them back out.

PS: Let me say you didn't really need me. You had it inside all along, couldn't you see? You're smart and so special, each one of you. I knew you'd be brave much more than you knew.

And so it was done the excitement of the day. Each bean now was happy with their fears tucked away. In the corner, they now had a new classroom pet. It was the best-behaved spider Ms. P had ever met.

About the Author

Tracy Stanaway is a retired dance teacher and mother of three children. She lives in beautiful Montana with her husband of thirty-five years. Her hobbies include playing the piano, singing, and traveling! This book and her first book, Jelly Bean Dean were written in memory of the original *Jelly Bean Dean*, Tracy's beautiful mom, Jerrine Dean. Jelly Bean Dean was her nickname all her life.